AFRICAN SAFARI

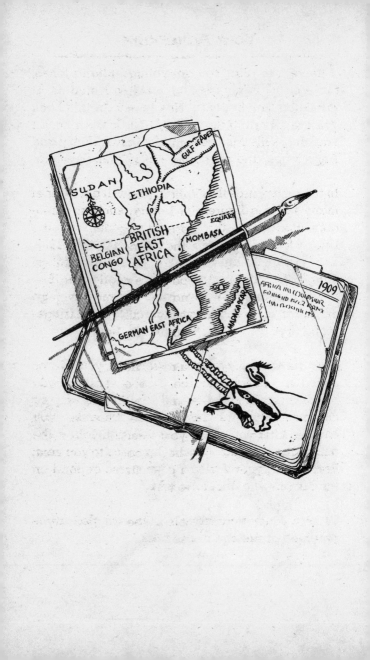

CAPTURED BY SAVAGE WARRIORS!

Suddenly, your friend Tomo lets out a cry of fear. Up ahead, lined across the road, is a band of natives in what could only be described as war paint. They are carrying long spears and huge shields. Their headdresses look like the manes of lions.

"Maasai!" Tomo gasps. "We're done for!"

Tomo tries frantically to turn the carriage around, but one of the Maasai warriors sprints forward and hurls his spear into the chest of your horse. The horse lets out a squeal of pain and drops lifeless to the ground.

You and your friend jump out of the carriage just as it topples over. You start to run, but you see right away that you're surrounded. What will you do?

ONLY *YOU*, AS YOUNG INDIANA JONES, CAN DECIDE. . . .

Bantam Books in the Choose Your Own Adventure® series
Ask your bookseller for the books you have missed

#1 THE CAVE OF TIME
#2 JOURNEY UNDER THE SEA
#3 DANGER IN THE DESERT
#4 SPACE AND BEYOND
#6 SPY TRAP
#7 MESSAGE FROM SPACE
#8 DEADWOOD CITY
#31 VAMPIRE EXPRESS
#52 GHOST HUNTER
#66 SECRET OF THE NINJA
#71 SPACE VAMPIRE
#77 THE FIRST OLYMPICS
#85 INCA GOLD
#88 MASTER OF KUNG FU
#92 RETURN OF THE NINJA
#93 CAPTIVE!
#95 YOU ARE A GENIUS
#96 STOCK CAR CHAMPION
#97 THROUGH THE BLACK
    HOLE
#98 YOU ARE A MILLIONAIRE
#99 REVENGE OF THE
    RUSSIAN GHOST
#100 THE WORST DAY OF
     YOUR LIFE
#101 ALIEN, GO HOME!
#102 MASTER OF TAE
     KWON DO
#103 GRAVE ROBBERS
#104 THE COBRA CONNECTION
#105 THE TREASURE OF
     THE ONYX DRAGON
#106 HIJACKED!

#107 FIGHT FOR FREEDOM
#108 MASTER OF KARATE
#109 CHINESE DRAGONS
#110 INVADERS FROM WITHIN
#111 SMOKE JUMPER
#112 SKATEBOARD CHAMPION
#113 THE LOST NINJA
#114 DAREDEVIL PARK
#115 THE ISLAND OF TIME
#116 KIDNAPPED!
#117 THE SEARCH FOR
     ALADDIN'S LAMP
#118 VAMPIRE INVADERS
#119 THE TERRORIST TRAP
#120 GHOST TRAIN
#121 BEHIND THE WHEEL
#122 MAGIC MASTER
#123 SILVER WINGS
#124 SUPERBIKE
#125 OUTLAW GULCH
#126 MASTER OF
     MARTIAL ARTS
#127 SHOWDOWN
#128 VIKING RAIDERS
#129 EARTHQUAKE!
#130 YOU ARE
     MICROSCOPIC
#131 SURF MONKEYS
#132 THE LUCKIEST DAY
     OF YOUR LIFE
#133 THE FORGOTTEN
     PLANET

#1 JOURNEY TO THE YEAR 3000 (A Choose Your Own Adventure
Super Adventure)

SPACE HAWKS™—

#1 FASTER THAN LIGHT
#2 ALIEN INVADERS
#3 SPACE FORTRESS
#4 THE COMET MASTERS
#5 THE FIBER PEOPLE
#6 THE PLANET EATER

PASSPORT—

#1 TOUR DE FRANCE
#2 FORGOTTEN DAYS
#3 ON TOUR
#4 PATH OF THE CRUSADERS
#5 MYSTERY ON THE TRANS-
   SIBERIAN EXPRESS
#6 MANHUNT

A CHOOSE YOUR OWN ADVENTURE® BOOK

THE YOUNG
INDIANA JONES
CHRONICLES™

Book 5
AFRICAN SAFARI

**BRITISH EAST AFRICA,
September 1909**

By Richard Brightfield

Adapted from the television episode
"British East Africa, September 1909"
Teleplay by Matthew Jacobs
Story by George Lucas

Illustrated by Frank Bolle

BANTAM BOOKS
NEW YORK · TORONTO · LONDON · SYDNEY · AUCKLAND

RL 5, age 10 and up

AFRICAN SAFARI

A Bantam Book / March 1993

CHOOSE YOUR OWN ADVENTURE® is a registered trademark of
Bantam Books, a division of Bantam Doubleday
Dell Publishing Group, Inc.
Registered in U.S. Patent and Trademark Office and elsewhere.
Original conception of Edward Packard

THE YOUNG INDIANA JONES CHRONICLES℗®
is a trademark of Lucasfilm Ltd.
All rights reserved. Used under authorization.

Cover art by George Tsui
Interior illustrations by Frank Bolle

ISBN 0-553-29953-0

Published simultaneously in the United States and Canada

Bantam Books are published by Bantam Books, a division of Bantam Doubleday Dell Publishing Group, Inc. Its trademark, consisting of the words "Bantam Books" and the portrayal of a rooster, is Registered in U.S. Patent and Trademark Office and in other countries. Marca Registrada. Bantam Books, 666 Fifth Avenue, New York, New York 10103.

PRINTED IN THE UNITED STATES OF AMERICA

OPM   0   9   8   7   6   5   4   3   2   1

Your Adventure

The year is 1909. You are young Indiana Jones, the son of a professor of medieval studies at Princeton University in New Jersey. In this book you are traveling through British East Africa, on vacation with your parents, Professor Henry and Anna Jones, and your tutor, Miss Helen Seymour.

In the adventures that follow, you will get to meet many famous figures in history, such as Theodore Roosevelt, the former president of the United States between the years 1901 and 1909. You will also experience life in the African savannah and learn all about the relationship between humankind and nature. You may even go on safari and locate the incredibly rare fringe-eared oryx and save it from extinction.

From time to time as you read along, you will be asked to make a choice. The adventures you have as Indiana Jones are the results of your choices. You are responsible because you choose. After you make your decision, follow the instructions to find out what happens to you next. Remember, your African adventures depend on the actions you decide to take.

To help you in your travels, a special glossary is provided at the end of the book.

You are Indiana Jones. You were born on July 1, 1899 in Princeton, New Jersey, where your father is a professor of medieval studies at the university. It is now 1909, and you are ten years old. You are traveling around the world with your parents. Also with you is your tutor, Miss Helen Seymour.

You are on a steamer heading down the east coast of Africa. In the preceding weeks, you left from the port of Marseille in the south of France, traversed the Mediterranean, and went through the Suez Canal. From there, you went down through the Red Sea and the Gulf of Aden into the Indian Ocean.

You are now somewhere off the coast of the African country of Somaliland heading south toward the port of Mombasa in British East Africa. You are standing with your tutor, Miss Seymour, gazing toward a thin strip of beach and distant surf sandwiched between a pale blue sky and a jade-green sea. The faint smell of spices is on the ocean breeze.

→ → → → → → → → → → → → →

Turn to page 2.

2

"This is the coast that Sinbad the Sailor sailed down in the *Arabian Nights*, bringing back jewels, ivory, myrrh, and frankincense to Baghdad," Miss Seymour says.

"I thought that was only a made-up story," you say.

"A story, yes, but it's true that the Arabs traded all along this coast, particularly for ivory and slaves," Miss Seymour says.

"Slaves?" you say.

"Oh, yes. The warrior tribes in central and southern Africa made a practice of raiding the peaceful tribes. They sold their captives to the Arabs and the Portuguese. Many of the captives were shipped as wretched and suffering cargo to the Americas, where they were forced to work as slaves on the plantations, particularly in the southern United States."

"That was a long time ago," you say.

"Not very long ago at all," Miss Seymour says, shaking her head. "There were still slaves in America when I was a little girl. Britain, of course, abolished slavery in 1833."

"Gosh!" you say. "I hope there aren't any slaves today."

"I'm afraid that there still are. Not in the United States anymore, but the Antislavery Society in England reports that the slave trade is still flourishing in Africa and the Middle East."

"That's awful," you say. "I wouldn't like to be a slave."

"I'm sure you wouldn't," Miss Seymour says. "Maybe when you are older, you can do something about stopping slavery where it still exists."

Just then, your father comes on deck, coming over to where you and Miss Seymour are standing.

"There you are, Henry," your father says, calling you by your given name. "We should arrive at Mombasa sometime tomorrow. From there, we'll take the Lunatic Express inland to Nairobi, then—"

"Lunatic Express? Good heavens!" Miss Seymour exclaims.

Your father laughs. "Don't be alarmed, Helen," he says. "That's just the nickname someone in the British Parliament gave it when the Uganda Railroad—its official title—was first proposed.

"It was, on the face of it," your father goes on, "an insane project considering the many obstacles that had to be overcome in order to build it. You'll see what I mean when we get there."

"Does your old school friend, the one who invited us to visit his coffee plantation, know that we're arriving?" Helen asks.

→ → → → → → → → → → → → →

Go on to the next page.

4

"I wrote him from Paris some time ago, but I have no way of knowing if he's received my letter," your father says. "Richard long ago gave us an open invitation to visit whenever we want. I'm sure he has plenty of room on the plantation."

"Does he have slaves?" you ask.

Your father laughs. "No, I don't think so. I'm sure the natives are quite happy to work for him. The British abolished slavery long before we did in the States."

"Well, that's enough about slavery for today," Miss Seymour says. "I think we should get back to studying our zoology books. I'm sure you'll want to know all about the many animals of Africa before we get there."

"You'll see plenty of them during our visit," your father says. "Africa has the largest concentration of wild animals left on earth."

That evening, after dinner, you and Miss Seymour decide to concentrate your studies on the antelopes. Miss Seymour turns the pages of a zoology book while you read the captions.

"It says here that the giant eland weighs up to a ton and stands six feet high. That's huge," you say.

"But look at this one," Miss Seymour says. "It's the royal antelope, only ten inches high."

"It says that there are over eighty species of all sizes," you say.

"Where do you think the word 'antelope' comes from?" Miss Seymour asks.

"I just read that . . . here it is, *antholope*, from the Latin, 'brightness of eye.'"

"Very good," Miss Seymour says.

"I don't think I'd like to be an antelope," you say. "It says here that they are the favorite food of lions, leopards, and a dozen other predators."

"I've heard that there are literally millions of them in gigantic herds, so your chances—"

"Wow!" you say. "Look at this one. It's beautiful."

"That's the fringe-eared oryx," Miss Seymour says. "Maybe you'll get to see one sometime soon."

"I hope so," you say. "I've never seen anything like it."

→ → → → → → → → → → → → →

Go on to the next page.

* * *

The next afternoon, your ship docks at the deep-water harbor of Mombasa. Nearby are hundreds of dhows, native sailing vessels, elbowing for room in this deep arm of the sea, their masts emblazoned with brightly colored pennants. High above looms a medieval fortress beneath which is a huddle of coral-stone houses, all painted tones of pink and tan. Off to the right, its main structure screened by acacia and baobab trees, is a small mosque. Its minaret rises above the town, a mixture of freshly painted buildings and graying ruins.

You step ashore with your parents and Miss Seymour, onto a wide dock piled high with bananas, stacks of ivory tusks, huge sacks of coffee beans, and large baskets filled with strange vegetables.

"I don't even know what some of these are," your mother says, examining some long tubers.

Several porters with faces of polished ebony are already loading your baggage onto a cart ready to be pulled by a group of men. Your father goes off for a few minutes and returns with a British official impeccably dressed in a white uniform and pith helmet.

"This is Mr. Campbell, the vice-governor of the territory," your father says. "He's arranged for us to stay in one of the government houses. It's on one of the highest points of the island."

→ → → → → → → → → → → → →

Go on to the next page.

"We're on an island?" you say.

"Quite so," Mr. Campbell says. "The island of Mombasa is about six square miles in area. It's separated from the mainland by a rather narrow creek, Macupa Creek, to be exact. Perhaps I can show you around the island later."

"That would be terrific," you say with excitement.

The government house is completely surrounded by a wide veranda, giving a view in all directions. Much of the town below is screened by exotic-looking trees.

"Those are acacia, palm, mango, and baobab trees for the most part," your mother says, coming out on the veranda. "And the flowers, what colors!"

Off in the distance you can hear the sound of a muezzin calling the Arab population of the town to prayer. It reminds you of Cairo and your stay in Egypt last year.

Early the next morning, you and your family have breakfast on the veranda.

"Your mother and I will be off for the morning, making arrangements for the train and shopping for things to take to the plantation," your father says. "Maybe you and Miss Seymour would like to—"

At this moment, Mr. Campbell arrives. "I couldn't help hearing your last statement, Professor Jones," he says. "I would like to make a couple of suggestions if I may." Turning to you and Miss Seymour he says, "We could take a walking tour of the Arab Quarter. There is no end of exotic sights there. Or we could take a jaunt around some nearby islands in my boat. The weather is perfect for a sail."

Miss Seymour and your parents leave the decision up to you. The tour of the Arab Quarter sounds exciting, but then so does the sailing trip.

→ → → → → → → → → → → → →

If you decide to take a tour of the Arab Quarter, turn to page 35.

If you decide to go sailing, turn to page 93.

You decide to go with Roosevelt on his safari. As your tutor, Miss Seymour is invited to go along as well. She is both excited at the idea and somewhat fearful of the dangers and hardships. However, she is relieved when she learns that the safari is taking along 260 porters and guides, dozens of wagons full of supplies, and sixty-four tents, one of which will be for her private use.

The evening before the safari is to leave, you, your parents, and Miss Seymour have dinner at the hotel. You are joined once again by Mr. Campbell.

"This safari sounds like a huge undertaking," your father says to Mr. Campbell. "I've been watching all the preparations going on in town."

"It is that," Mr. Campbell says. "Roosevelt plans to collect and salt down the skins of hundreds of animals for your country's Smithsonian Institution in Washington. I understand that he's already shot two hundred and ninety-six animals, including nine lions, ten giraffes, eight elephants, three rhinos, and half a dozen buffalo."

"Heavens!" your mother says. "Why, he's slaughtering all the animals."

→ → → → → → → → → → → → →

Turn to page 36.

Later, you and Miss Seymour meet up with your parents. After a late lunch on the veranda of Government House, the four of you board a kind of trolley. It's on tracks and pulled by several men, and you take it back to the dock. Mr. Campbell meets you there. He is also going to Nairobi on government business.

"The train will leave shortly, at precisely eleven A.M.," he says. "It's due to arrive in Nairobi at eleven-fifteen tomorrow morning, though I must say that our time of arrival is somewhat less predictable than our time of departure."

The train is drawn up a short distance from where you landed after your voyage. Your ship is unloading supplies, which in turn are being speedily transferred to the baggage cars of the train.

"Your president Theodore Roosevelt landed here five months ago during the rainy season— in a fantastic downpour," Mr. Campbell says. "Poor chap was drenched to the skin by the time we got him to Government House. He took it all with great humor, I must say."

"Roosevelt is heading up an expedition to gather specimens for the Smithsonian Institution, I believe," your father says.

"I wonder if we'll see him?" Miss Seymour says.

→ → → → → → → → → → → → →

Go on to the next page.

"There's a good chance. I've heard that he returns to Nairobi between his various safaris. Oh, and speaking of Roosevelt," Mr. Campbell says, turning to you, "we rigged up a seat on the cowcatcher on the front of the train for him. I wonder if you'd be interested in riding that way too."

"I sure would," you say with excitement.

"Then jump aboard," Mr. Campbell says, pointing across to the front of the locomotive. "Think I'll have a try at it myself."

You go over and climb aboard the cowcatcher. Mr. Campbell takes a seat beside you. Miss Seymour and your parents decide to ride inside the train.

The train whistle gives several shrill blasts, lets out a hiss of steam, and lurches forward suddenly.

"I think you're going to like this ride," Mr. Campbell says. "I was told that your president referred to it as a journey back to prehistoric times, when humans were a new species and survival depended on what nature provided."

"My father called it the Lunatic Express," you say.

→ → → → → → → → → → → → →

Go on to the next page.

"And rightly so," Mr. Campbell says. "The government in London felt it was needed to transport soldiers to Lake Victoria at the headwaters of the Nile River, five hundred and eighty miles from here. It seemed simple enough for the planners in London to draw a line on the map, but when it came to laying the tracks, that was something else. The laborers put down railroad ties soaked in a preservative, creosote. But the white ants ate the railroad ties anyway."

You listen to Mr. Campbell's story as the train slowly chugs its way across the bridge over Macupa Creek to the mainland. Then, with smoke and red-hot embers pouring from its smokestack, the train picks up speed and rattles through a long stretch of palms on both sides of the track.

"You see," Mr. Campbell continues, "there was nothing west of Mombasa at that time except for a primitive trail laid down by Arab traders. The country was virtually unexplored. The builders had to punch through three hundred miles of gradually rising scrub country, fighting malaria, sleeping sickness, and even the attacks of some man-eating lions. But the real test came with the country west of Nairobi, a town that didn't really exist at that time. There they encountered the Great Rift valley, a fifty-mile-wide ditch thousands of miles long, with eight-hundred-foot walls on both sides."

"How did they get over that?" you ask.

Go on to the next page.

"It wasn't easy, I can tell you," Mr. Campbell says.

The train struggles up a steep incline, heading toward the hills to the west.

"We're lucky that the weather is dry," Mr. Campbell says. "When it rains, the dust on the track turns into a slippery mud that makes the wheels lose traction. Then we'd be lucky to get over these hills at all."

"I'm beginning to see why they call this the Lunatic Express," you say. "With all those difficulties, only a lunatic would try to build it."

After a few hours, the land levels off. The train begins to make frequent stops, sometimes to load water and firewood for the boilers, other times to let passengers get on or off.

Then, coming around a curve, you see a herd of zebra on the tracks. The train comes to a sudden, screeching halt.

→ → → → → → → → → → → → →

Go on to the next page.

16

The conductor runs out, waving his arms and shouting, trying to shoo the zebra off the tracks. The zebra run a few yards away, then turn to stare at the tracks.

The conductor returns to start the train up again. At the same time, Mr. Campbell goes back to see how your parents and Miss Seymour are doing.

Suddenly, you notice that a young zebra is stuck on the tracks up ahead, its hoof apparently caught on something. When the train starts moving again, it might get run over. You feel you should run up there and see if you can help the young zebra get loose. On the other hand, you know that you're not supposed to leave the train.

→ → → → → → → → → → → → →

If you decide to run up and try to help the zebra, turn to page 105.

If you decide to run back and tell the engineer, turn to page 49.

You decide to follow Meto to his village. Halfway there, he stops and looks back to see if you are coming. He smiles broadly, flashing brilliant white teeth, when he sees that you are.

When you get to the village, Meto pulls open a thornbush "gate" and shoos the goats inside. Then he closes it again. He points over to some rocks in the shade of a nearby acacia. On the way over to the umbrella tree, he places a thin stick upright in the ground.

Soon you find yourself sitting on one of the rocks, with both of you throwing pebbles at the stick several yards away. Meto's aim is remarkable—he hits the stick many times. But you can't seem to hit it at all.

After a while, you open your journal and show Meto the sketch of the oryx that you made from your zoology book. Then you pantomime searching for it with your hand cupped over your eyes. Meto laughs and gestures for you to follow him again as he jogs toward another ridge some distance away.

You run after him, but by the time you reach the other ridge, you are completely out of breath. Meto is not even breathing hard. He goes up the side of the ridge in a crouch, gesturing for you to do the same.

→ → → → → → → → → → → → →

Turn to page 50.

Once inside the bungalow, you're not sure what you are eating, but the food doesn't taste all that bad. The main problem is fighting off the clouds of mosquitoes swarming around you.

As you try to eat, you tell Miss Seymour and your parents what it was like to ride on the front of the train. "It's like going through a weird kind of dream," you say. "But it's really real out there. It's beautiful."

After dinner, everyone gets back on the train and climbs into upper and lower berths for the night.

You wake up early the next morning and realize that the train has stopped again. You get dressed in your berth and go out onto the platform. One of the porters hands you a bun of some sort and a cup of strong tea.

"We'll soon be on the plains for the final run to Nairobi," Mr. Campbell says, coming up behind you. "This is the really interesting part."

As the train starts up again, you take a seat next to Mr. Campbell in the railway car and look out the windows on both sides. A short time later, you realize what Mr. Campbell meant about this stretch being interesting. Way off to the south is the snow-covered peak of Mount Kilimanjaro, rising out of its garland of clouds. To the north are the jagged peaks of Mount Kenya, also snow covered. It's strange to be so near the equator and see snow, you think.

Go on to the next page.

* * *

Sometime later, you begin to pass small houses, each in its own grove of trees. Then you come to a stop in the train station of Nairobi. Mr. Campbell looks at his watch.

"My, that must be some kind of record," he says. "Only two hours late. Usually we're a dozen hours behind schedule, sometimes a whole day. I trust you enjoyed the ride."

"I sure did," you say.

You and Mr. Campbell walk down the platform of the long brick station with its large clock tower at the center. There you meet your parents and Miss Seymour, who are waiting for you.

"Did you know that Nairobi means 'place of cold water' in the Maasai language?" Miss Seymour asks you.

"Right you are," Mr. Campbell says. "A strange name for a jumbled mixture of unlikely houses and shacks along dry, dusty streets. But we're advancing very rapidly. We have a number of impressive government buildings constructed of stone, as well as several hotels and a hospital. On the religious side, we have a number of churches, some mosques, and even a Hindu temple."

"Very impressive," Miss Seymour says. "Especially since what we consider civilization has only recently come to this part of Africa."

→ → → → → → → → → → → → →

Go on to the next page.

Your mother thanks Mr. Campbell for taking you around.

"The pleasure was mine," Mr. Campbell says, turning to shake your hand. "I trust I will see more of all of you while you are in Nairobi. And now, if you'll excuse me, I have some business to attend to."

You watch as Mr. Campbell goes back down the platform. There he turns his attention to a long row of oxcarts that are being loaded with supplies from the train.

A horse-drawn wagon pulls up next to the platform where you are standing, and your father directs the loading of your heavy baggage into it.

"You, Helen, and Junior can go to the hotel, while I finish up here," your father tells your mother.

Junior! You always hate it when your father calls you that.

"All right, Henry," your mother says. She heads over to a line of human-powered rickshaws that are lined up near the station. You and Miss Seymour follow.

"Why don't you take that one?" Miss Seymour tells your mother. "We'll take this one over here."

As soon as you climb in, Miss Seymour says, *"Tafadhali Norfolk Hoteli"* to the man pulling the rickshaw.

"I'll bet that's Swahili," you say.

"Right you are," Miss Seymour says. "I told him

to take us to the Norfolk Hotel. I hope he understands me."

Whether he does or not, the rickshaw starts off at a rapid pace, then proceeds to bounce along the main thoroughfare, a wide, unpaved street lined with tall, neatly spaced trees. The one carrying your mother is close behind.

The rickshaws soon pull up to a two-story stone building with a red-tiled roof. You, your mother, and Miss Seymour all check into the hotel and go to your rooms. There you unpack the small suitcases you are carrying.

When you are finished you go back down to the wide veranda at the side of the hotel just in time to meet your father.

"I have good news," he says. "President Roosevelt is expected back from a two-week safari this afternoon. A reception is going to be held for him this evening at the governor's house. Furthermore, we're all invited!"

"Won't Mr. Roosevelt be exhausted after being out in that wilderness for weeks?" your mother says. "You'd think he'd need a day or two to rest."

"Not Teddy Roosevelt," your father says. "He's full of boundless energy."

"Will I get to meet him?" you say.

"I'm sure you will," Miss Seymour says.

"Oh boy!" you say.

→ → → → → → → → → → → → →

Go on to the next page.

*   *   *

Later, at twilight, you and Miss Seymour take a rickshaw. Your parents follow behind in another one as you head to the governor's house. The house is a smaller version of your hotel, located at the end of a long, tree-lined driveway and surrounded by gardens bursting with brilliantly colored flowers.

You go inside and over to the dining room where tables have been arranged to form a large, hollow rectangle. They are covered with embroidered tablecloths and the finest china. Native waiters in spotless white jackets are hurrying back and forth from the kitchen, placing bowls of food on the table.

You, Miss Seymour, and your parents take your places at the table. Your father is dressed in his formal dinner jacket with a white tie. Your mother and Miss Seymour are both wearing their best white blouses and floor-length skirts. The rest of the guests are also formally dressed.

The waiters place dishes with large slices of steak in front of each of you. You wait until everyone starts eating and take a few bites.

"This is pretty good," you say.

"I believe it's one of the specialties of Nairobi," your father says. "Gazelle steak."

Your fork stops in midair.

→ → → → → → → → → → → → →

Go on to the next page.

"Gazelle steak?" you say. "You mean we're eating one of those beautiful animals?"

"Cows are just as beautiful to some people," your father says. "Anyway, you saw how many there are from the train. They are the main prey of all the carnivores around here, including humans."

You finish your steak, but you don't enjoy it as much as you had before. You wish your father hadn't told you what it was.

Suddenly there is a flurry of activity outside. A few seconds later, a solidly built man strides in. His round face is set off with a bushy mustache and steel-rimmed spectacles, and topped with a shock of brown hair. You instantly recognize President Roosevelt from the many pictures you've seen of him.

→ → → → → → → → → → → → →

Turn to page 61.

Deciding to tell President Roosevelt where the oryx are, you crawl outside your tent by way of the back flap. The camp is quiet. Everyone seems to be asleep—except for a light coming from the president's tent. You go over quietly and look inside. Roosevelt is surrounded by mosquito netting and is writing furiously at a small table.

You cough slightly at the tent flap, and Roosevelt looks up.

"Ah," he says. "I thought you were supposed to be in bed. What can I do for you?"

"I hope you're not mad at me for what happened today," you say.

Roosevelt laughs. "Not really. You had me worried, but I'll confess that it's just the sort of thing I did at your age."

"I know where the fringe-eared oryx are," you blurt out.

"You do?" Roosevelt says, half standing up.

"They're in a small valley about a four-hour hike from here. I saw them. And I think I've figured out why they're not around this area anymore."

→ → → → → → → → → → → → →

Turn to page 62.

"This is a new country of unlimited horizons," Roosevelt continues. "I compliment you all on your pioneer spirit."

Another round of applause goes up after these statements.

For a while after that, Roosevelt is uncharacteristically silent, concentrating on his food. The room resumes its normal conversation. Then Roosevelt gets up and quietly slips out the back door of the dining room.

Soon the banquet breaks up and people start to leave.

"I think we can be getting back to the hotel," your father says.

"I didn't really get to meet Roosevelt," you say.

"Maybe tomorrow," your mother says.

"Such a splendid man," Miss Seymour says, as you file out the front door of the house. Your father shakes hands with the governor just outside, thanking him for the dinner.

You, Miss Seymour, and your parents then head toward the row of rickshaws lined up further down the road. The gardens on either side are now bathed in the light of a half-moon in a cloudless sky.

Partway down one of the narrow paths that thread through the gardens from the road, you see a tiny creature, its eyes glowing in the moonlight. At first sight you think it might be some kind of dog. But then you realize that it's a gazelle—one of the tiny ones. Without a second thought you run down the path after it.

"Come back here!" Miss Seymour shouts. But you are already a good way down the curving path.

→ → → → → → → → → → → → →

Go on to the next page.

Suddenly, you collide with a large figure. Looking up, you see that it's President Roosevelt.

"Gee, I'm sorry," you say.

"Quite all right," Roosevelt says. "I just saw a small gazelle dart into the woods. I assume that you were chasing after it."

"I . . . was," you say.

"They are very fast. Perhaps, though, if you had a gun, you could have brought it down. Do you shoot?"

"I'd never shoot a gazelle," you say. "They're beautiful creatures."

"They are, I agree. But there are literally millions of them and there's certainly no danger of them becoming extinct," Roosevelt says. "They are an essential part of the food chain for dozens of animals."

"I guess you're right," you say.

"Bully for you," Roosevelt says. "And now I'd better be getting you back to your parents."

You and President Roosevelt emerge from the gardens just as Miss Seymour and your parents are about to come looking for you. Your father introduces everyone properly. Roosevelt shakes hands heartily with all of you. Miss Seymour nearly faints when he shakes her hand.

→ → → → → → → → → → → → →

Go on to the next page.

Roosevelt, it turns out, is staying at the same hotel you are. He suggests that you and your father walk back to the hotel with him. Miss Seymour and your mother decide to take a rickshaw.

Your father and Roosevelt get along famously, trading stories of their travels all the way back to the hotel.

"It's as though the prehistoric age of the Pleistocene had come to life again here," Roosevelt says.

"I feel that way too," your father says. "Have you read the works of Charles Darwin?"

"I certainly have," Roosevelt says. "In fact, I have a copy of his *Origin of Species* in my kit along with thirty-seven other books I selected for the trip, including Mark Twain's *Huckleberry Finn* and Bret Harte's *Luck of Roaring Camp*. They're all bound in jungle-proof pigskin. I'm never without my library wherever I go."

"Admirable," your father says. "Then you must know that Darwin believes this part of Africa could be the birthplace of humankind."

"Yes, a very interesting theory. It could just be," Roosevelt muses. "The various primitive peoples I've run into here are all worthy of study—and respect, I might add." Roosevelt then turns to you. "I hope you have a chance to study them as well as the animals and plants."

You're glad that you're finally being noticed. You thought they had all but forgotten about you.

"I'm leaving on a new safari in a couple of days," Roosevelt says to you. "Perhaps you would like to come along—with your father's permission, of course."

"Thank you for the offer, Mr. President," your father replies. "Junior and I will discuss the matter and let you know."

"You don't have to decide right away," Roosevelt says. "Any time before I leave will be all right."

You and your father say good-night to Roosevelt and then go up to your rooms. "I know this safari is a great opportunity to see what big-game hunting is like," your father says. "On the other hand, you may not like it that much. They intend to kill a lot of animals, and I know how you feel about hunting. Besides, my friend Richard and his wife Karen have been looking forward to meeting you. They will be very disappointed if you don't visit them. I think you'll find their coffee plantation as exciting in its own way as the safari. Still, I will leave the decision up to you. Whichever you choose will be all right with me."

→ → → → → → → → → → → → →

Go on to the next page.

You spend the next couple of days trying to decide what to do. You don't want to disappoint your father and his friends. But then again, you don't want to miss this chance of going on a real safari, especially with the president of the United States.

← ← ← ← ← ← ← ← ← ← ← ← ←

If you decide to go with President Roosevelt on his safari, turn to page 10.

→ → → → → → → → → → → → →

If you decide to go to your father's friends' coffee plantation, turn to page 66.

You decide to take a tour of the Arab Quarter.

You say good-bye to your parents, then Mr. Campbell takes you and Miss Seymour through the maze of narrow, shaded lanes of the quarter. They open out in all directions into sun-drenched squares, some filled with stalls selling tomatoes, beans, lemons, mangoes, guavas, and oranges. In the side streets, carpenters are busy making furniture of teak and cedar in open workshops. They remind you of the open markets you saw in Cairo.

Many of the natives call out *"jambo bwana"* to Mr. Campbell as you walk by.

"What language is that?" you ask.

"That's Swahili for 'Hello, Sir,'" Mr. Campbell says. "It's an ancient language fashioned by the Arab traders centuries ago—a mixture of the Bantu languages and Arabic. It became the *lingua franca*, or universal trading language, of East Africa. When you consider that there are over seven hundred tribal languages here, you can understand that it was really needed. It is, as you can see, still used today."

← ← ← ← ← ← ← ← ← ← ← ←

Turn to page 11.

Mr. Campbell laughs. "I dare say, Madam, that it's like taking a cup of water out of the ocean and worrying about the ocean drying up."

"I'm sure President Roosevelt would not kill more than is necessary for his scientific studies," Miss Seymour says.

"But someday, there might not be so many," you say. "What about the elephants? I saw huge piles of tusks on the dock where we landed at Mombasa. Don't they have to kill the elephants to get their tusks?"

"Good point. I'll have to admit that there's a problem there," Mr. Campbell says. "The demand for ivory is tremendous. We should start some kind of conservation effort before the ivory hunters decimate the elephant herds." He then turns to you. "Maybe you could keep an eye out for anyone killing a large number of elephants for their tusks," he says.

"I'll write in my journal about anything that I see," you say.

"Very good," Mr. Campbell says. "Maybe you can give me a report when you get back."

"Above all, be careful," your mother tells you.

"I will," you say. "I promise."

Early the next morning, an hour before dawn, the safari moves out like a small army into the high, open scrubland west of Nairobi. President Roosevelt and his twenty-year-old son, Kermit, ride on horseback at the head of the column. You and Miss Seymour, also on horseback, follow the wagon train.

For the next several hours the safari moves at a steady pace across the landscape. Just before noon, Roosevelt spots a small herd of unidentified antelope in the distance. The caravan is stopped while Roosevelt, his son, and a number of gun bearers gallop ahead to try to collect some specimens.

In their absence, several cook tents are set up to prepare food for the midday meal.

"I'm going to try to find a place where I can wash up a bit," Miss Seymour says. "I'm already covered with dust from the trail. You stay close to camp while I'm gone."

"Yes, Miss Seymour," you say, trying to look like you wouldn't *think* of wandering off.

Way off to the right is a fairly high ridge in the mostly flat terrain. You wait until Miss Seymour is out of sight, then head for it. When you get there, you find a great view from the top.

A sea of tall grass stretches endlessly to the west, dotted here and there with the flat-topped acacia—which everyone seems to call "umbrella trees." On the horizon to the north is the white-tipped Mount Kenya, now appearing closer than you've seen it before.

→ → → → → → → → → → → → →

Go on to the next page.

Directly below you, not very far away, is a small village of mud huts built in a circle and surrounded by a fence of thornbushes. You look at it for a while, but you don't see any people or any movement inside. Your guess is that it's deserted, at least for now.

You are about to turn and go back to camp when you notice a small native boy about your own age nearby. He is standing very still on one leg, his other leg bent behind him. He's holding on to a long stick, the end of which is firmly planted in the ground.

You wave to him, but his face remains expressionless. The two of you stare at each other for a while. Then you walk toward him down the other side of the ridge, pointing to yourself.

"My name is Indy," you call out. "I . . . Indy." Then you point your finger in his direction, hoping that he will understand that you are asking him his name.

The boy lets out a shrill cry and raises his arm to his face as though to ward off invisible bullets from your finger. You realize that your gesture is scaring him for some reason. You'll have to try something else.

Suddenly a native appears from the direction of the village. "Meto! Meto!" he calls out.

The boy turns and calls back in his own language. Then he heads toward the village.

→ → → → → → → → → → → → →

Go on to the next page.

"Meto!" you call out.

The boy looks back in surprise. That must be his name, you realize. You wave good-bye and head back toward camp.

Roosevelt's hunting party doesn't return until late in the afternoon. Kermit, the president's son, comes back first with a team of porters carrying the bodies of the animals that their hunting party has killed. The porters take them directly to the taxidermy tents.

Meanwhile, Kermit begins to set up a camera tripod at the western edge of camp, handing an assistant a flashgun.

Kermit then mounts a large camera on the tripod and aims it down the trail. A few minutes later, you see President Roosevelt riding in on horseback. When he gets closer, he calls out to Kermit, "Are you ready?"

"Yes, Dad. All set."

You watch in amazement as President Roosevelt rides in against a background of the setting sun and the picturesque African bush. The flashgun goes off, and Kermit has another "heroic" picture of his father.

Later, after the evening meal, you and Miss Seymour find yourselves in the envious position of sitting around the campfire with the president and his son.

→ → → → → → → → → → → → →

Go on to the next page.

"I'm really proud of Kermit," Roosevelt says. "He shot a rhino today at point-blank range, then took some excellent photos of the carcass."

"Why don't you just photograph the animals instead of killing them?" you ask.

"Now that's not a proper question to ask," Miss Seymour says.

"No, that's all right. It's a fair question," Roosevelt says. "In the first place, there are not many animals out here that will sit still long enough to have their pictures taken."

"For many of the animals I do just take photographs—when I can," Kermit says. "But Dad has promised to bring back specimens that can be stuffed and placed in museums for everyone to see. It brings the animals to people who might not otherwise have a chance to see them and helps give people a greater understanding and appreciation of nature."

"It also helps the naturalist to identify and catalog many unknown species," Miss Seymour says. "There seem to be many different kinds of antelope, for example."

"That's true," Roosevelt says. "For the antelope, so far we've collected specimens of bohor, sing-sing, oribi, lelwel, kob, and even the very rare bongo."

"Some we haven't even identified yet," Kermit says. "I guess we'll have to leave that up to the zoologists back home."

"One that we still haven't found is the fringe-eared oryx," Roosevelt says. "I promised the Smithsonian I'd bring one back."

"I know about the oryx. There's a picture of one in my zoology book. I even made a sketch of it in my journal," you say.

"Do you have it with you?" Roosevelt asks.

"I have it back in my tent," you say. "I'll go get it."

You dash back to your tent and quickly return with both books. You hand them to Roosevelt. He reads over the text in the zoology book carefully.

"You see. This book clearly indicates this area as being one of the main breeding grounds of the fringe-eared oryx," Roosevelt says. "There should be thousands of them around here."

"Let me take a look at that," Kermit says.

Roosevelt hands the book to his son, who turns back to the front of the book.

"My guess was right, Dad," Kermit says. "This book was published a number of years ago. It's out-of-date."

"That may be," Roosevelt says. "But they couldn't have just all died out like that."

"Perhaps they migrated south," Miss Seymour says. "I've been told that this has been a fairly wet season. I remember reading that the oryx prefer dry areas."

"Yes, you may have something there," Roosevelt says. "I can see that you are quite a student of—"

Roosevelt is interrupted by a series of growls from somewhere far off in the darkness.

"A lion!" Kermit says.

"Definitely a lion," Roosevelt says. "The roar of a lion can be heard for six or seven miles. Nothing to worry about."

→ → → → → → → → → → → → →

Go on to the next page.

There is a mumble of sounds from a group of native porters sitting around a nearby campfire. Then they begin to chant softly in unison. You wonder if they are trying to magically keep the lion away or if they are just using the chant to overcome their fears.

"Lions, contrary to their bad reputations, will seldom attack humans unless they are under attack themselves or realize that they are being hunted," Roosevelt says. "They dislike the taste of humans and find the odor of humans repugnant. They will usually run away if they smell you coming."

"But I've heard about lions killing people," you say. "When they were building the railroad they—"

"I know all about that," Roosevelt interrupts. "There have been a few what I would call renegade lions. Usually they are ones that have become lame or too old to hunt antelope. They have to settle for what they can get."

You notice Miss Seymour shudder at the thought. Then you hear the roar of the lion again—this time it sounds a bit closer. You see Miss Seymour turn slightly pale. "Do you think this one will attack us?" she says.

"Not likely," Roosevelt says. "Of course, I don't want to make everyone feel too complacent about lions. Lions can weigh over four hundred and fifty pounds and charge at thirty-five to forty miles per hour. I shot one once that measured nine and a half feet from the tip of its nose to the end of its tail. They are so strong they can drag away a zebra that would take almost a dozen men to lift."

"And they're almost invisible in the tall grass," Kermit says. "They can sneak right up just a few yards away and then charge like an express train. You're lucky to get off a shot even if you have your gun at the ready. And one shot won't usually stop them."

There's another roar, this time much closer. The natives start to chant louder. Kermit picks up his rifle and checks to see that it's loaded.

"Well, time to turn in," Roosevelt says. "That lion could go on roaring all night. At least we know where it is. When it stops, we'll start worrying. I have sentries posted, so don't worry. As for me, I have my good-luck piece—a gold-mounted rabbit's foot."

President Roosevelt and his son go off to their tents. Then you and Miss Seymour start toward yours.

"Can I . . . just for tonight—" you start to say.

"Yes," Miss Seymour says. "You can set up your bedroll in my tent."

Later, you pull the blankets up over your ears and shut your eyes tight. Still, it's a long time before you fall asleep.

→ → → → → → → → → → → → →

Go on to the next page.

*   *   *

Early the next morning, Roosevelt and Kermit leave on another hunt. They've decided to keep the base camp where it is for the time being while they go off to bring back more valuable specimens, which will then be skinned for shipment back to the States.

After breakfast, you decide to go back out to the ridge and see if you can find the native boy called Meto. Sure enough, he's there again, this time tending a few goats.

You wave and call out his name.

Meto waves back and calls out, "In-dy." You can't believe he remembers!

Then he gestures for you to follow him as he drives the goats back toward the village below. You hesitate for a moment. You're not sure if you should go that far away from camp. What if Miss Seymour catches you?

On the other hand, you don't want to miss the opportunity to become friends with one of the natives—especially one your own age. You'd like to get to know what the people in Africa are like, and how they live. Also, he may know where there are some fringe-eared oryx.

← ← ← ← ← ← ← ← ← ← ← ← ←

If you decide to follow Meto, turn to page 19.

→ → → → → → → → → → → → →

If you decide to go back to camp, turn to page 82.

You decide to run back and tell the engineer about the young zebra stuck on the tracks.

"What?" the engineer says. "Not another of those crazy animals stuck again. Don't worry, the cowcatcher will knock it off the tracks."

"But you can't just run over it, it's . . . inhuman," you say.

"All right," the engineer says. "But I'm not letting you ride on the cowcatcher anymore if you're gonna keep causing trouble."

"I don't care," you say. "I'm not going to let you kill that poor animal."

The engineer and several other men reluctantly go up the tracks. After much effort, they finally free the zebra, and it goes limping off. You spend the rest of the trip riding inside the train, sitting with your parents and Miss Seymour.

In the late afternoon, a brilliant sunset spreads across the sky. The train stops at a small bungalow next to the tracks.

"This is where we have dinner, I believe," your mother says.

← ← ← ← ← ← ← ← ← ← ← ← ←

Turn to page 20.

At the top of the ridge, you raise your heads carefully to see what's on the other side. Nearby is a water hole with a number of animals at its edge, drinking. There are several giraffes, some elephants, and hundreds of white birds swirling about. But no fringe-eared oryx.

Then suddenly you see the head of a lion, just down at the bottom of the slope, gazing up in your direction. Both you and Meto duck your heads and start to back down your side of the ridge.

You get down to the bottom and quickly start back across the plain, when the ground starts to vibrate under your feet. Before you can look around, Meto pulls you down under a fallen log. Seconds later, a herd of wildebeest stampedes past you, some leaping over the log above your heads. The ground shakes all around you.

As the last of the wildebeest charge by, you and Meto crawl out from under the log. Meto begins talking away in Maa, his native language. You start to repeat some of his words, trying to imitate his pronunciation. He begins to point out things like the sky, the grass, and the trees, teaching you the words in his language.

For a long time you sit there while Meto teaches you a basic vocabulary. You then try to do the same for Meto with English. Later, Meto seems to indicate, "We go find oryx in picture. First, we go see the Laibon. He is very wise."

Go on to the next page.

Meto leads you back toward his village. When you are close to it, you follow him up a small hill with a beautiful tree on top. You can hear the melodic sound of a flute coming from somewhere. It takes you a moment to realize that it's being played by a very old man sitting on the other side of the tree.

Meto kneels down in front of the old man and makes a kind of salute with his hands. You can see that Meto has great respect for him. This must be the Laibon Meto was talking about.

Meto places your drawing of the oryx in front of the old man. They talk in Maa. You've learned just enough to more or less make out what they're saying. "Fringe-eared oryx, where?" Meto asks. "My friend searches for them."

→ → → → → → → → → → → →

The Laibon thinks for a second, then carefully sweeps the dirt in front of him until it is smooth. He reaches for a twig and draws what looks like a ball on the end of a stick. He looks up at you. "Melon," he says in Maa. "Very good to eat."

"Melon, very good to eat," you repeat in Maa.

The Laibon next draws pictures of a rat and a snake. He says the word for fire in Maa and crosses out the snake. Then he crosses out the melon. Both Meto and the Laibon try to explain what they mean. Your head is swimming. All you want to do is find the oryx. In any event, you copy all the information down in your notebook.

Meto leads you away from the Laibon and the village. "We go now and look for fringe-eared oryx itself," he says as you go across another few miles of scrubland.

Finally, you reach a very steep rock face. You follow Meto as he starts to climb up. It's not an easy climb. You have to watch him closely to see where he gets handholds on the rock.

→ → → → → → → → → → → → →

Go on to the next page.

You are both about halfway up when you see the head of a mean-looking black snake at the spot where you were just about to put your hand! You hate snakes, and you can't help crying out in fear. The snake hisses and rears back, ready to strike. You hang there, frozen with fright.

Meto looks down and sees your predicament.

"Don't move!" he calls out as he grabs a fist-sized stone from the cliff face. With a graceful motion, he lets it fly, all the while hanging onto the cliff with just his other hand. The stone smashes the head of the snake against the rock. You duck as it bounces over your head. The snake, still alive and wriggling, goes flying off into space.

You cling to the rock face for another few minutes, still shaking like a leaf. Meto reaches down and helps you climb up to a ledge near the top.

"That bad kind of snake," Meto says in his language.

→ → → → → → → → → → → → →

Go on to the next page.

Meto leads you the rest of the way up the cliff. You follow him for another hour, moving from scrub country up into the foothills of the mountains. You are amazed that Meto can travel such long distances without showing any signs of fatigue.

Finally you come out on a rocky precipice that looks down on a small, enchanted valley. Meto leads you down a trail to the valley floor. All around you are the tall stalks of a distinctive plant of some kind. Meto starts digging at the foot of one of the plants and comes up with a hard, melon-sized root. "Root-melon!" he says, proudly holding it up. "Food for oryx—you will see."

Meto finds a rock nearby and cracks the melon open. It has a reddish fruit inside. "Now we wait," he says, going off to the side of the valley and crouching behind some bushes.

You wait for a little time. Meto is the first to see one. He nudges you with his elbow and points to a single oryx gingerly emerging from the bush. It is followed by three others. The first oryx walks over to the broken melon and starts eating. The others start digging for more with their hooves.

You and Meto sit there mesmerized—watching the small herd of oryx.

"It is getting late," you say in English. "I'd better be getting back."

Meto looks at you, puzzled.

"We . . . return," you say in his language.
"Yes, return," he says.

It is almost dark when you get back to Meto's village. You say good-bye and run back toward the safari camp in the growing darkness. You are beginning to get scared. The shadows of the bush create frightening shapes. Once or twice you are convinced that there are lions crouching in wait. Several times you stumble.

→ → → → → → → → → → → →

Suddenly you are grabbed by a large, dark figure and lifted off your feet. You are too scared to cry out.

"*Jambo bwana kidogo*," a deep voice says. It is one of the porters from the camp. "Hello, little one."

The porter puts you down and you both walk toward the campfire in the distance up ahead. He calls out to several figures grouped around it. One of them is Miss Seymour. She jumps up and runs over, grabbing and hugging you.

But you can tell that she is really upset, particularly when she takes you by the shoulders and shakes you.

"Don't ever, ever do that again," she says. "We've been worried sick."

President Roosevelt comes up behind her.

"You've caused a lot of trouble around here," he says. "We've had all the porters out beating the bush to find you."

"But . . . I—" you start.

"No excuses," he says. "You've had your tutor in a state of panic the entire day. She was sure you'd been eaten by lions."

"Sorry."

"So you should be," Miss Seymour says. "And furthermore, you are going straight to bed—and no supper for you either."

→ → → → → → → → → → → → →

Go on to the next page.

"I'm sorry," you say. "I was just trying to find the oryx, and I—"

"You heard what the president said," Miss Seymour interrupts before you have a chance to finish.

Later, by the light of a small lamp that you sneak under your covers, you go over the notes in your journal about the fringe-eared oryx. Then you read the section about it in your textbook. It says that the oryx favors a hard, melon-shaped underground root, often called the "elephant's football." You remember the Laibon drawing a picture of a rat and then a snake. You're still not sure what it all means, but you're beginning to piece things together.

Should you tell President Roosevelt where the oryx are? you wonder. He may just go out and shoot them. But maybe if he only shot one for scientific purposes it would be all right. It's a hard decision. The oryx is such a special animal, you'd hate to see anything happen to it.

You try to decide what would be the proper thing to do, but you're not so sure.

← ← ← ← ← ← ← ← ← ← ← ←

If you decide to tell President Roosevelt where the oryx are, turn to page 27.

→ → → → → → → → → → → →

If you decide not to tell him, turn to page 87.

Everyone stands and applauds as Roosevelt takes the seat of honor at the head of the tables. Immediately he dominates the conversation in the room.

For most of the dinner, everyone—particularly Miss Seymour—hangs on his every word. "In America, I've placed one hundred and twenty-five million acres of forest land in national parks," he says. "I consider this the crowning achievement of my administration. J. P. Morgan, that old millionaire, doesn't like this at all. He thinks all the forests should be cut down for firewood for his railroads. When he heard I was coming to Africa he said that he hoped the first lion I encountered would 'do its duty.' Well, I can tell you that the lions that tried it are now being stuffed and will soon be on display at the Smithsonian Institution."

Roosevelt laughs heartily at his joke, joined by you and the rest of the diners.

"And I must say," Roosevelt goes on, "your highlands here resemble the West of my country, particularly Wyoming, Colorado, and parts of New Mexico and Arizona. Indeed, there is a lot here that is like the American Wild West."

← ← ← ← ← ← ← ← ← ← ← ←

Turn to page 28.

"Why is that?" Roosevelt asks.

"Well, you see, the oryx dig up and eat this kind of root-melon," you say. "I was thinking. There must have been this great fire that killed all the snakes. The snakes usually eat the mole-rats, but they must have burrowed underground and not been killed by the fire. With no snakes to eat the mole-rats, the rats multiplied and ate all the root-melons. No root-melons, no oryx, it's as simple as that."

"I'd hardly call that simple," Roosevelt says. "But what you say makes sense. Anything that happens to one animal causes things to happen to other animals. It's the balance of nature. Now, you say you know where some of the surviving oryx are? In a valley, you say."

"That's right."

"Then we'll be off in the morning to see these oryx of yours. They may be our prize specimens."

"Do you think you could shoot only one?" you say. "They're a pretty rare species."

"Right you are," Roosevelt says.

Early the next morning, you, President Roosevelt, and Kermit saddle up and ride toward the valley. It takes a while to find a way around the cliffs that you and Meto climbed the day before.

Finally, you see the valley below. The three of you dismount, tie up your horses, and head down on foot. Roosevelt and his son have their guns ready.

"You're sure that this is the place where the oryx are?" Roosevelt asks.

"Yes," you say. "If we're quiet, they'll come out."

Roosevelt and Kermit settle down behind some rocks. You wait for a long time. You can see that Roosevelt and his son are getting restless.

Then the oryx slowly start to emerge from the bush, one by one.

Roosevelt and Kermit both fire at the same time. Two of the oryx are hit immediately. Roosevelt is about to fire again when you leap over and push the barrel of his gun away from the line of sight of the animals.

"You said just one," you shout.

Kermit, also about to fire again, lowers his rifle with a confused look on his face.

"That's enough, Kermit," Roosevelt says. "One *is* enough. Two, actually, counting yours. They are a rare species. When we get back, I'll send out a party to collect these specimens."

When you get back to camp, you find out that Miss Seymour has decided that you and she should return to Nairobi. Her nerves are still in a state of collapse from your disappearance the day before.

Accompanied by Miss Seymour, you go out to the ridge to say good-bye to Meto. But he is not there, and the village is really deserted this time. The tribe has moved their flocks to different pastures, and Meto must have gone with them.

"I'll never forget him," you tell Miss Seymour as you stand on the ridge.

"Farewell, my friend," you shout in Meto's language. The sound echoes out across the hills as you start back toward camp.

The End

You decide to go with your parents to the coffee plantation. The evening before you are to leave, your parents invite President Roosevelt and his son Kermit to join all of you on the veranda of the hotel. Roosevelt is busily preparing for his safari, but he finds a few minutes for a farewell meeting.

"It's been a pleasure knowing you and your charming wife," Roosevelt tells your father and mother. He then turns to you. "I'm sorry that you're not joining me on the safari, but I realize that accompanying your father to the plantation means a lot to you. I respect your decision. And I certainly enjoyed meeting you, Miss Seymour. I have a feeling that we'll all meet again in some other part of this great world. We're all adventurers."

Roosevelt has certainly become one of your idols. As you say good-bye, you wonder if you made the right decision. By now, however, you realize it's too late to change your mind.

Early the next morning, not long after Roosevelt's safari has moved out of town like a military operation, you, Miss Seymour, and your parents climb into the back of a large wagon with a canvas roof. Then you head out of town yourselves on a broad, dusty dirt road.

"It's a good thing we're making this trip now and not a few months ago," the wagon driver says. "Then we would have been sunk in mud higher than our wheels."

After going for several hours, you start up into the rolling Ngong Hills, a parklike countryside with patches of forest alternating with stretches of grassland.

Finally you pull up in front of a rambling stone farmhouse. It has a large sloping roof of corrugated metal.

Your father's friend, Richard Medlicot, and his wife, Karen, run out to meet you. Your father and Richard pat each other on the back enthusiastically, and Karen and your mother give each other a big hug. After that, you and Miss Seymour are introduced.

"It's too bad that our children are grown and back in England going to school," Karen says. "There are no really proper schools out here yet."

"That's one reason why we brought Miss Seymour along on the trip," your mother says, looking at you.

"Not that there's a lack of things to learn about around here," Karen says to you. "I suggest that you and our native girl, Kuma, become friends. She's your age and she speaks English quite well. She can help you to speak some Bantu and learn about the cultures of the different tribes around this area."

→ → → → → → → → → → → →

Go on to the next page.

"Excellent idea," your father says. "I think Helen needs a good rest, anyway."

Miss Seymour nods with relief.

"Here is Kuma now," Karen says.

A small girl in a white smock comes out of the front door of the farmhouse. She has very fine, coffee-brown features and a high, rounded forehead. Her head is covered with a scarf.

Karen introduces the two of you.

"Very glad to meet you," Kuma says, turning her head shyly to one side.

"Kuma will be free of all her kitchen duties while you are here, so she can show you around any time you wish."

"Right now sounds good," you say.

"Splendid," Richard says.

Kuma takes you out to the fields, where a long, neat row of sparkling-green coffee bushes covers the gentle slopes of the hills.

"When the fields redden with ripe berries," Kuma says, "all the people of my tribe will come to pick them. The Medlicots are very kind. We are glad to work for them."

"Mrs. Medlicot said you could teach me some Bantu," you say. "I'm keen on languages."

"That would be nice," Kuma says. "Perhaps you can visit my village. It's not so many miles from here."

→ → → → → → → → → → → → →

Go on to the next page.

That night, at dinner, you ask the Medlicots about visiting Kuma's village.

"Yes, that could be arranged," Richard says. "A short visit perhaps."

"There's no trouble with the natives, is there?" your mother asks.

"No, not at all," Richard says. "The Kikuyu for the most part are peaceful and industrious. I must say that they take to civilization like ducks to water. The future of Africa is in the hands of people like them."

A few days later, it's arranged for you to visit Kuma's village. You and Kuma are to be accompanied by Tomo, one of the Medlicots' most trusted workers.

Tomo drives you along a bumpy trail to the village in one of the plantation's horse-drawn carriages. The village turns out to be a collection of many small, round, stone houses, each with a tall, conical, thatched roof. Flocks of chickens are running between them. Patches of cultivated land, growing beans, sweet potatoes, and pumpkins, surround the village.

The people of the village run out to greet you and Kuma as the carriage arrives. Most of the women of the tribe are covered from their heads to just above their knees in masses of multicolored beads. Some of them have large loops in their ears, filled with huge earrings.

You spend several hours in the village, meeting the people and learning their customs. After a while, though, Tomo starts getting nervous. He has heard rumors in the village that there are Maasai, a tribe of merciless raiders, in the hills. He talks to Kuma.

"We must start back for the plantation," Kuma says.

"Trouble?" you ask.

"Maasai raiding parties from far to the south have been seen," Kuma says. "It may not have been wise to come here."

"But if your people are in danger . . . "

"They are, but they are prepared to defend themselves," Kuma says.

You, Kuma, and Tomo leave the village in the carriage and head back for the plantation.

"Can you teach me some more words in your language?" you ask Kuma.

"You see over there—Mount Kenya," Kuma says. "That is our sacred mountain, the home of God, or *Ngai* in our language. The word 'kenya' means ostrich in Bantu."

→ → → → → → → → → → → → →

Go on to the next page.

You are about to ask why the mountain was named after an ostrich when Tomo lets out a cry of fear. Up ahead, lined across the road, is a band of natives in what could only be described as war paint. They are carrying long spears and huge shields. Their headdresses look like the manes of lions.

"Maasai!" Tomo gasps. "We're done for!"

Tomo tries frantically to turn the carriage around, but one of the Maasai warriors sprints forward and hurls his spear into the chest of your horse. The horse lets out a squeal of pain and drops lifeless to the ground.

You, Kuma, and Tomo jump out of the carriage just as it topples over. You start to run, but you see right away that you're surrounded.

The Maasai raiding party forces you, Kuma, and Tomo off the main dirt road and on to a narrow path into the hills.

"I speak a little of their language," Kuma says. "Maybe I can reason with them."

"It's worth a try," Tomo says.

"We are from the coffee plantation," she calls over. "They will come after you with guns and kill you if you harm us or do not let us go."

The warriors let out a series of fierce shouts and shake their spears in the air. One of them calls back in the Maasai language.

→ → → → → → → → → → → → →

Go on to the next page.

"What did he say?" you ask Kuma.

"He said Ngai will protect them from the white man's bullets."

"Well, I guess that approach didn't work," you say.

"Yes, we must find a different way," Tomo says.

"What will they do with us?" you ask him.

"They will sell us as slaves to the Arab traders," Tomo says. "I think that's why they haven't just killed us."

"I'm not sure of that at all," Kuma says. "Many of the Maasai are peaceful herders. It's only the moran, the warriors, who rob and kill."

"But our captors are moran," Tomo says, now shaking like a leaf.

"Most of the Maasai only eat milk, butter, and blood," Kuma goes on.

"Blood!" you say.

"From their cattle," Kuma explains. "They use the point of a sharp arrow to puncture the veins in the cattle's necks, then they drink the blood. They never eat the meat of the cattle or the meat of any wild game, though I hear they hunt animals for sport."

"Interesting people," you say sarcastically.

The moran march you along for hours. Finally, you come to a Maasai settlement, a circle of crude mud huts surrounded by a fence of thornbushes. Several of the moran herd you inside the compound and over to the front of one of the huts.

A strange-looking young man ducks out of the low doorway and stands in front of you. His body is completely covered with a red clay that makes him look more like a statue than a human. Otherwise, he is wearing a black and white fur cape over his shoulders, a headdress of ostrich and vulture feathers—and little else.

"That's a young Laibon, an apprentice priest of the tribe," Kuma whispers to you.

"He looks more like a witch doctor to me," you whisper back.

→ → → → → → → → → → → → →

Go on to the next page.

The Laibon walks slowly around the three of you several times, looking you over carefully. Then he sits cross-legged in front of his hut and throws several pebbles on the ground like dice.

"That's the way the Laibon predicts the future," Kuma whispers.

The Laibon stands and turns in the direction of Mount Kenya. He raises his arms, chanting something in the Maasai language.

"Mount Kenya is their sacred mountain, as it is with our tribe," Kuma says. "Ngai, the supreme god, husband of the moon, and creator of all things, lives there."

Then the Laibon turns back to the three of you—and smiles! Then he says something in his language.

Both Kuma and Tomo looked relieved.

"He says that the moran have made a mistake. They will let us go. But first we must go with them on a lion hunt so that we can see the bravery of the warriors."

The Laibon lets out a high-pitched cry, and a number of women come out of the huts. They are all wearing strings of beads around their heads, their arms, and their waists. They too are wearing little else.

→ → → → → → → → → → → → →

Go on to the next page.

The women form a circle at the side of the compound and start to chant and clap their hands. The warriors who were guarding you jump into the circle and start bouncing up and down to the rhythm. Their hands are held rigidly at their sides while they do this, whereas the women rock back and forth to the beat.

Other warriors come from just outside the village and join in the dance. Then, at a command from the Laibon, the warriors stop and line up in single file. They trot out of the village, shaking their shields and spears up and down. The Laibon gestures for you to follow.

You, Kuma, and Tomo run along behind them. You could make a run for it, but you're afraid the warriors would just turn and come after you.

After traveling several miles, the warriors slow down and start to move forward cautiously. A scout, running ahead, has apparently spotted a lion nearby. The warriors fan out across the fields on both sides of the trail. Then they start to form a large circle, closing in on the lion at the center.

You keep a safe distance back from the closing circle of warriors, but you are still close enough to see all the action.

The lion walks defiantly out of the bush, shaking its mane and growling contemptuously at the warriors.

→ → → → → → → → → → → → →

Go on to the next page.

As the warriors tighten their circle, the lion begins to sense its danger. Its mane bristles and its tail lashes back and forth. Finally, the lion charges the warrior closest to it.

The warrior braces himself behind his shield as the other warriors let out bloodthirsty cries and charge in from both sides.

As the lion hits the shield, it knocks the warrior backward to the ground. The lion digs its long fangs into the warrior's shoulder. At the same time, the other warriors thrust their long spears into the sides of the lion, some of them going completely through.

The lion lets go of the fallen warrior and grabs a spear in its jaws, bending it double before falling lifeless to the ground. The warriors from the opposite side of the circle all arrive and thrust their spears into the dead lion.

The wounded warrior is lifted to the shoulders of the others like a football hero and carried back to the Maasai village. He seems happy enough about the whole thing, and none the worse for his injury.

Back at the village, the Laibon assigns a guide for the three of you. Your guide leads you back to the coffee plantation.

When your father hears the whole story, he says, "I suggest you stay close by the plantation until we leave."

Somehow, you agree with him.

You and Kuma spend a lot of time studying Bantu. It's a language you've really started to enjoy. When the time comes to leave, you are genuinely sad to leave your new friend.

As your wagon leaves the plantation, Kuma, Tomo, and the Medlicots wave good-bye. Your trip to Africa is an experience you'll never forget.

The End

You decide to return to camp. You wave goodbye to Meto and head back down the ridge.

When you get there, you sense an air of excitement. Miss Seymour sees you and comes running over.

"There you are!" she says. "I've been looking all over for you. Mr. Thornby, a famous ivory hunter, just arrived in camp. He says that there's a large herd of elephants not far from here. He's going out to investigate and we're invited to go along. Mr. Thornby assures me that there's absolutely no danger as long as we keep our distance from the herd."

"Is he going to shoot the elephants for their tusks?" you ask.

"Well . . . I don't know," Miss Seymour says. "I expect he may shoot one or two. But that's his business now, isn't it?"

"I'm not so sure," you say.

A short time later, a native porter brings two horses around to your tents—one for you and one for Miss Seymour. Both of you mount up and ride over to a small column of riders and porters on foot, led by Mr. Thornby just as they are starting off. Mr. Thornby himself, a somewhat overweight man in khakis and a pith helmet, comes over and rides beside you and Miss Seymour.

"Jolly good to have the two of you with us," he says, as you ride out of camp.

You cross a grassy plain for an hour or so, keeping a careful watch for lions. After that, you plunge into dense woods. The trail is barely passable for a while, then it breaks out into a wide, tunnellike path.

"A herd of elephants passed through here quite recently," Mr. Thornby says. "They trample down a quite passable trail. The woods and jungles are riddled with their paths. You might say that the elephants are the pioneer road builders for this part of the world."

"They are interesting animals," Miss Seymour says. "I understand that their trunks are extensions of their nose and upper lip."

"And they can pick up water with their trunks," you say.

"Quite right," Mr. Thornby says. "Two gallons at a time. They also use their trunks to breathe and smell, of course. They can't see too well, but their senses of hearing and smell are very acute."

"I would imagine those huge ears of theirs are good at picking up sounds," Miss Seymour says.

"Ah, yes," Mr. Thornby says. "And that's why we must be very quiet when we find the herd."

The column stops. A rider comes back and tells Mr. Thornby that the herd of elephants should be just up ahead. You and the others dismount and tie up your horses. Then you proceed cautiously on foot.

→ → → → → → → → → → → → →

Go on to the next page.

Up ahead, the elephant trail opens up into grassland again. You see a herd of forty or fifty elephants, accompanied by a huge flock of birds—white egrets. The elephants are grouped around a water hole, noisily gurgling the water and trumpeting with their trunks.

Mr. Thornby signals for everyone to stop at the edge of the woods and keep undercover. He calls up his gun bearer and takes hold of a huge rifle.

"Too far away to get a good shot," he whispers. "I'll have to get closer. Everyone stay here and be very quiet."

Keeping as low a profile as possible, Mr. Thornby creeps forward, trying to get the elephants in range.

While everyone is watching Mr. Thornby, you carefully slip off to the side where no one can see you. You find a stone about the size of a baseball and pitch it as high as you can through the trees. It makes a loud, crackling sound, snapping off small branches as it arcs through the trees.

The egrets, startled, all take to the air in a swirling flurry of activity. The closest elephants let out sounds almost like screams. Then the whole herd stampedes off in the other direction.

You quickly slip back behind Miss Seymour. Luckily, no one has noticed that you were gone.

→ → → → → → → → → → → → →

Go on to the next page.

Mr. Thornby comes back, very disappointed. "What luck!" he says. "Must have been one of those crazy monkeys. They're all around here. It would have to scare the elephants just when I almost had one in my sights."

Not this time, you say to yourself. You're glad you saved at least one elephant from being killed.

"Well, they're going too fast for us to catch up with them today," Mr. Thornby says.

The hunting party makes its way back to camp. You go back happy, satisfied that you've done your good deed for the day—at least for the elephants. You realize your father was right about the safari. All this killing of animals, many of them helpless to defend themselves, makes you mad. You wish you could do more to stop the killing. Maybe someday you will.

The End

You decide not to tell President Roosevelt where the fringe-eared oryx are. He is liable to go out and kill them all. You put your journal away and turn off your lamp.

As you sink into a deep sleep, you dream of being an antelope yourself. No lion or leopard can catch you, because you can run like the wind across the plains.

The bright sun through your tent flap wakes you up the next morning. While you get dressed, you can hear all sorts of activity going on outside.

A few minutes later, as you walk over to the cook tent for some breakfast, you see that the tents are being taken down and packed up. The safari is getting ready to move further into the wilderness.

"Oh, there you are," Miss Seymour says, arriving at the cook tent. "I've just been told that we're going to explore the bottom of the Great Rift."

"Mr. Campbell was talking about the rift on the train," you say. "He said it was the hardest section to put the railroad across."

"I can well believe that, from what I've heard about it," Miss Seymour says. "It looks like we're now going to get a chance to see for ourselves."

→ → → → → → → → → → → → →

Go on to the next page.

The safari moves off into a dry, brown semi-desert with only a scattering of trees and thorn-bushes. Later, you camp for the night in a desolate area surrounded by volcanic craters.

Early the next morning, you start off again. Soon you come to the edge of the rift, a vast depression in the earth's surface. The view is overwhelming. The land drops almost straight down in front of you for thousands of feet. Before you is a huge valley stretching almost as far as you can see. The other side is dimly seen through the mists, and you can see the glint of a lake far below.

"That's Lake Naivasha down there," Kermit says, riding his horse up next to yours. You are glad for this chance to be with Kermit. Up until now, you've mostly just seen him dashing around, busy with his photographic equipment. "Dad expects to bag a hippopotamus down there. *Kiboko*, the natives call them. I hope I can get some good photographs."

As the safari starts down the very steep trail that leads to the valley far below, you ride beside Kermit. By late afternoon, you are on the floor of the rift and camping at the edge of a large, shallow lake.

You and Miss Seymour listen while President Roosevelt and Kermit plan their strategy.

"The hippos are way out in the lake marshes," Roosevelt says. "We'll use the rowboat that we brought along."

"But Dad, I can't set up my camera in a small boat," Kermit says.

"You'll have to wait until we can pull a dead one ashore," Roosevelt says.

"But those hippos are huge," Kermit says. "And the guides tell me that their skin is almost bulletproof."

"But a precise shot into the brain—" Roosevelt starts.

"Heavens!" Miss Seymour exclaims.

"Remember, it's all for science," Roosevelt says.

"Of course," says Miss Seymour. But you can see that, like you, she feels slightly sick at the idea.

Miss Seymour has decided to stay behind. You sit tight at the back of the boat as Kermit rows it through the reeds and shallow water. President Roosevelt stands at the bow, his rifle cradled by his left arm.

"Over there, Kermit," he says. "I saw some movement in the water."

Seconds later, a hippopotamus surfaces, spouting a stream of water up into the air. Roosevelt takes aim and fires.

"Did you get it, Dad?" Kermit asks.

"I'm not sure, I . . ."

→ → → → → → → → → → → → →

Go on to the next page.

Suddenly the hippopotamus rears up, opening its huge mouth. It charges toward the boat, its gaping jaws open. It looks as if it's going to swallow the boat and all of you with it in one gulp! Roosevelt has just enough time to reach down, pick up a shotgun at his feet, and fire into the open jaws of the animal.

The jaws clamp shut just inches from the bow of the boat and sink partway into the water.

You gaze at it in shock for a few minutes.

"The beast is definitely dead," Roosevelt says finally.

"That was a close one, Dad," Kermit says.

"Let's get back," Roosevelt says. "I'll have the porters come out and tow it ashore."

The thing you'll remember most about this trip, you think, is seeing the gaping jaws of the hippopotamus coming at you. There will be many more adventures to come, but this one will always be impressed on your mind.

Africa has certainly been an exciting place—one you'll never forget.

The End

You decide to go sailing.

You say good-bye to your parents, then leave with Mr. Campbell. He takes you and Miss Seymour to the "Old Harbor" on the east side of the island.

"This port is used mostly for dhows and smaller craft," Mr. Campbell says. "I keep my thirty-three-foot ketch, *Victory*, tied up here. It's named after Lord Nelson's flagship at the glorious Battle of Trafalgar. I'm sure that you, Miss Seymour, being British yourself, can appreciate that."

Miss Seymour smiles and nods approvingly.

Victory has two masts. The main one, toward the front of the boat, carries the mainsail and two jibs. A smaller mast toward the stern has a smaller, triangular sail. Two British sailors in uniform standing on the deck salute smartly as you, Miss Seymour, and Mr. Campbell go aboard.

"This is seaman Wilson and seaman Pruit," Mr. Campbell says, introducing them to you.

"There's a quite ample cabin below, Miss Seymour," Mr. Campbell says. "I think you'll find all the . . . amenities, if you need them."

The seamen cast off the mooring lines, and Mr. Campbell takes the wheel just behind the smaller mast at the stern.

→ → → → → → → → → → → → →

Go on to the next page.

There's a good breeze blowing across the harbor. Soon the boat is out in the open ocean under full sail. *Victory* heels over to one side as the wind fills her sails and her bow cuts through the water. The two seamen take positions at the bow, ready to adjust the sails when needed.

The island of Mombasa, with its green hills, pink minarets, and massive gray fort at its highest point, quickly recedes.

"Are we going very far out?" Miss Seymour asks.

"Not very far," Mr. Campbell says. "Just to some islands nearby. It's too bad we don't have time to go further out to the Amirantes. Those are idyllic coral islands with sparkling lagoons. To the east of these is the high, mountainous island of Mahé. Since 1903, all of these islands, well over a hundred, have been incorporated into the crown colony of the Seychelles."

Soon you are running close to the shore of an island somewhat smaller than Mombasa. A small Arabic town with a mosque at its center fills a peninsula at the far end. A tiny harbor is crowded with dhows.

"It's about time to head back," Mr. Campbell says, steering the boat in a wide arc to the south.

Up ahead on the horizon, a gray, leaden curtain has fallen over part of the sky, though it's still clear overhead.

"Looks as if we could be in for a bit of a blow," Mr. Campbell says. "Never fear, though. *Victory* is a tight ship. I'll have Wilson and Pruit shorten sail if need be."

Soon you begin to see flashes of lightning, followed by the low rumble of thunder. You can see the slanting sheets of rain in the strip between the ocean and the clouds.

"A storm like this is a bit unusual this time of year," Mr. Campbell says. "It's a bit frustrating when they hang off the coast like this, considering there's a drought onshore."

Suddenly a very strong wind whips across the water, turning the surface into churning whitecaps. Pruit and Wilson struggle to get the sails down before the wind capsizes the boat.

"I suggest we go below," Mr. Campbell says. "The crew can handle things topside."

You, Miss Seymour, and Mr. Campbell struggle down the ladder that leads into the cabin. The ship is being tossed around like a cork, and you have to hold on to something for balance to keep from being tossed from side to side.

The storm goes on for hours. The ship groans and shudders as waves crash over it. Loud and ominous wrenching sounds come from above.

Eventually the storm dies down, and the ocean seems calmer.

"I'm going topside. You wait here until I get everything under control, then you can come up," Mr. Campbell tells you and Miss Seymour.

→ → → → → → → → → → → → →

Go on to the next page.

After a few minutes, Mr. Campbell comes back, ashen faced.

"I'm afraid I have a bit of bad news," Mr. Campbell says. "Our masts and sails are gone, and the crewmen are missing."

"Oh, my!" Miss Seymour says. "Those poor men."

"They still have a chance," Mr. Campbell says. "They were wearing life jackets. Fortunately there are numerous—"

Suddenly there is a terrific jolt and a terrible grinding sound under the boat. Jets of water start shooting up from the floorboards.

"Numerous islands, I was going to say," Mr. Campbell says. "And reefs. Unfortunately, I think we just hit one."

The three of you rush topside. The deck is a mess. Only frayed stumps are left of the masts, and the rope railings that once ran around the ship have been stripped away.

Not far away, on the other side of the reef that the ship just hit, is a low-lying island. There you can see a long, glistening-white beach and a grove of palm trees in the distance.

There are more grinding sounds, as the waves rock the ship back and forth on the reef.

"Do you think we could swim to shore?" you ask.

→ → → → → → → → → → → → →

Go on to the next page.

"It would be very dangerous," Mr. Campbell says. "If we got caught on the sharp, jagged reef, we could be cut to pieces. However, there is a small dinghy lashed down to the deck near the bow. Fortunately, it wasn't washed overboard in the storm."

The three of you run to the front of the boat. There Mr. Campbell quickly cuts the ropes tying the dinghy to the deck with a seaman's knife he keeps sheathed to his belt. You and Miss Seymour help as he pulls the dinghy to the side of the deck, then overboard, carefully securing it with a rope. After you all climb inside, Mr. Campbell pushes off from the rapidly sinking *Victory*. Then he detaches two small oars from the inner sides of the dinghy.

"It's now a matter of timing," Mr. Campbell shouts over the sound of the surf breaking on the reef. "We have to wait until there's a particularly big wave and . . . here comes one now."

Mr. Campbell struggles with the oars, trying to catch the wave with the dinghy. He does, and the three of you are carried over the reef on top of the wave. The dinghy settles gracefully into the calmer, shallow water inside the reef. You then wade ashore, with Mr. Campbell pulling the dinghy behind him.

→ → → → → → → → → → → → →

Go on to the next page.

As you sit on the beach, you wonder what you'll do now. Looking over at the reef, you see no sign of the ship. It has vanished into the ocean.

"I wonder how big this island is," you say.

"Not very big, I imagine," Mr. Campbell says. "But we won't really know until we explore, will we?"

The main part of the island turns out to be about two miles long and a little more than half a mile wide. There's a large, shallow lagoon on the other side of the island, surrounded by a bare, narrow beach. There are also several groves of coconut palms. Other than that, you see only a lot of ants, a lot of birds, and lots and lots of small lizards.

"Unfortunately, these palm trees are very old," Mr. Campbell says. "The fronds are yellowish, and they have about one coconut apiece, if they have one at all. Still, we won't starve. Those large birds out on the sand spit are boobies. We can eat either the birds or their eggs. There are also abundant fish in the lagoon, I'm sure, if we can figure out how to catch them. And there are hundreds, if not thousands, of these small lizards."

"Are you suggesting that we eat lizards?" Miss Seymour says.

"Oh, yes," Mr. Campbell says. "They're quite tasty, once you get used to the idea of eating them. Their skin is a bit rubbery, but the insides are delicious."

"Only as a last resort, Mr. Campbell," Miss Seymour says.

"I don't think it will come to that," Mr. Campbell says.

Later, you find an old abandoned hut at the center of the island. It's raised on stilts and has a thatched roof, though the roof is badly in need of repair. Best of all, you find a fishing net inside.

"This must have been a small coconut plantation at one time," Mr. Campbell says. "I'm not surprised that they abandoned it. What little soil there is here is of poor quality."

That night, Mr. Campbell lights a driftwood fire on the beach with the flint he always carries in his pocket. He also managed to save the knife he used on the deck of his boat. Miss Seymour borrows it to deftly clean a fish you caught in the lagoon with the net from the hut. Later Mr. Campbell borrows the knife back to open a few coconuts so that you can drink the "milk" inside.

→ → → → → → → → → → → → →

Go on to the next page.

"Well, here we are, cast away on a desert island like Robinson Crusoe," Mr. Campbell says.

"You remember that story, don't you?" Miss Seymour asks you.

"It's one of my favorites," you say. "I hope we don't have to wait twenty-eight years to get rescued like he did."

"Heavens, what a thought! How long do you think it *will* take?" Miss Seymour asks Mr. Campbell.

"A week perhaps. A month? It's hard to tell," Mr. Campbell says. "One thing I do know, they'll jolly well be out looking for us."

As it happens, it does take several weeks for you to get rescued.

Miss Seymour does her best to make the abandoned hut seem like a home, while Mr. Campbell does a passable job of fixing up the roof. You become quite good at finding birds' eggs as well as climbing up the trees for coconuts. There are actually a lot more of them than Mr. Campbell thought. The coconut milk is a good thirst quencher. You also find that you can sip small amounts of seawater from the lagoon, as long as you don't drink too much.

Finally, a passing ship sights one of your nightly fires. A boat is sent for you in the morning over the reef at high tide.

When you get back, your parents are naturally quite happy and relieved. They stayed in Mombasa, and never lost faith that you were safe and would soon be found. You are also glad to learn that Mr. Campbell's crewmen, Wilson and Pruit, were picked up by a passing ship at sea. They survived the storm and are doing all right.

Your father's schedule, however, was thrown way off, and you all lost the chance to visit his friend's coffee plantation. Even without that experience, you'll never forget the days you spent on the island.

The End

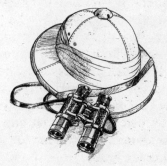

You decide to try to rescue the young zebra. You jump off the cowcatcher and dash down the tracks. The zebra is still struggling to free itself when you reach it, out of breath. You can see right away what's wrong. A railroad tie has split into two pieces, and the zebra's hoof is trapped between them.

Fortunately, a two-foot-long metal bar, probably left by a worker, is lying nearby. You use it to pry open the split just enough for the zebra to pull out its hoof.

Suddenly the train blows its whistle a couple of times. The shrill sound panics the mixed herd of zebra and wildebeest nearby, and they start to stampede across the tracks. They dash by all around you.

You start to run back to the train, but a wildebeest almost runs you down. You jump back to get out of its way and bump into the young zebra you freed. It's still standing there on the tracks.

Suddenly you see another wildebeest charging in your direction. Almost without thinking, you grab hold of the mane growing from the young zebra's neck and pull yourself up onto its back.

You get away just in time. The wildebeest thunders over the spot where you were just standing. This frightens the zebra, and it starts running—with you still clinging to its back!

→ → → → → → → → → → → → →

Go on to the next page.

The zebra heads away from the tracks toward a wide, open expanse to the south. There are thousands of galloping animals on all sides of you. Their hooves thunder on the ground. You can't jump off, or you'll be trampled to death.

You hear the train whistle blow again. It's far off in the distance now behind you.

The herd slows down a bit from time to time, but just when you think you're going to slip off the zebra and start back toward the railroad, something spooks the herd, and it goes charging off again—with you still part of it.

Fortunately, the zebra you are riding doesn't seem to mind having you on its back. Maybe it understands that you freed it from the trap on the railroad tracks.

The vast herd is now trotting along. After a while, you notice that it's growing dark out. The sunset is beautiful, but you are too scared to enjoy it. You are afraid of what will happen when it gets really dark.

What if the zebra you are riding on is attacked by lions? you wonder. Then you realize that there are thousands of zebra and wildebeest around you, stretching for as far as you can see. The chances of any lion singling you or your zebra out are very slim.

Night falls, and you are now in total darkness, except for the bright stars overhead. Suddenly you are sinking. You feel a moment of panic, but then you realize that the zebra is just kneeling down on the ground.

The herd is hushed, but you can feel that all of the animals are still ultra-alert. In the distance, you hear all sorts of strange cries—the trumpeting of elephants way off, and closer, the roar of a lion on the hunt. You also hear other sounds that could be hyenas, giraffes, or leopards.

You slip down off of the zebra's back and feel relaxed enough to lie next to it. Somehow, you manage to drift off to sleep for a few hours. When you wake up in the first gray light of dawn, your zebra is still kneeling beside you patiently. Its eyes are open, and it's looking around intently, sniffing the morning air.

You reach over and rub the zebra behind its ears, the way you did with your dog, Indiana, back in the States. The zebra snorts softly and makes a noise that sounds like a sigh.

Soon you notice that the herd is getting restless. The animals that were kneeling or lying down are now starting to get up. Your zebra does too, and once again you quickly slip onto its back.

As the sky grows lighter, you see a small lake in the distance. The herd starts cautiously toward it.

→ → → → → → → → → → → →

Go on to the next page.

When you get closer, you can see elephants splashing around in the shallow water near shore. Further out in the lake are some animals with long, sloping horns that you guess are African buffalo. Way out, you see a herd of hippopotamuses in the deeper water. Only the very tops of their backs, their eyes, and their ears are above the water. On the other side of the lake, a huge herd of antelope is moving toward the water.

Your zebra takes you down to the edge of the lake, where it lowers its head to drink. The water looks pretty muddy to you. As thirsty as you are, you don't think you can face drinking any of it.

After quenching its thirst, the herd breaks up into smaller groups, which move off to stretches of grass. They start munching on it happily as you look around, taking in your surroundings. The sun is now high in the sky—and hot.

You climb down from your zebra. You can't resist patting it on the head and saying good-bye. From the look in its eyes, you feel it somehow understands what you are saying.

→ → → → → → → → → → → →

Go on to the next page.

You go over to a nearby baobab tree and jump up on a branch that droops down almost to the ground. Fortunately, it's on the shady side of the tree. You are hungry and thirsty, but you don't want to start hiking over the countryside in the heat. As you sit there watching the vultures circling in the sky, you hope they don't have your number.

By late afternoon, your muscles are sore from clinging to the branch for so long. You are about to climb down when you see a group of horsemen in the distance coming toward the lake. You recognize one of them—it's Mr. Campbell!

"I'm over here!" you shout. They hear you and gallop in your direction.

"Well, see what you get for running with the herd," Mr. Campbell says as you ride behind him on his horse. Then he laughs. "I'll bet this is one adventure you'll never forget."

You take another swig of water from his canteen.

As you ride back to the train to Nairobi, you take a last look around. Mr. Campbell is right—this *is* one adventure you'll never forget.

The End

Glossary

Africa—The second-largest continent after Asia, Africa is 5000 miles from north to south, 4700 miles from east to west, and has 23,000 miles of coastline. European exploration and invasion of Africa began in the 1770s. By the early 1900s, European countries, with military superiority, had claimed and seized large parts of Africa for their own colonial expansion and exploitation.

Antelope—A large deerlike animal with hoofs and hollow horns. Most species of antelope live in Africa. They survive by running away from their enemies—mostly lions—at high speeds. The fringe-eared oryx is a rather rare species of antelope.

Baobab tree—An African tree that has an oversized trunk—from thirty to fifty feet in diameter. It is often called the "upside-down tree" because its stunted-looking branches resemble exposed roots. The trunk of the baobab is soft and usually full of holes dug by birds and small mammals. The bark is also a favorite food of elephants.

British East Africa (now called Kenya)—A country in East Africa on the Indian Ocean. It is one of the most populous in Africa, with more than forty ethnic groups, the largest being the Kikuyu. The Arabs traded along the coastline here for centuries but were afraid to go very far inland because of the fierce raiding parties of the Maasai. In 1890, the British established the protectorate of British East Africa and subdued the Maasai to some extent, making settlement possible. The protectorate became the crown colony of Kenya in 1920. In the late 1950s and early 1960s, the country was besieged by the Mau Mau revolt against European control, with the revolutionaries coming from the Kikuyu tribes. In 1963, Kenya became fully independent.

Elephant—Second in size only to whales, elephants are the largest land animals. The nose of the elephant has evolved into a long trunk that it can use like a hand. Elephants have many almost-human qualities—they form long-lasting friendships with each other and greet each other by touching trunks and rubbing shoulders. Grass is their most important food, but they love fruits and will eat almost any kind of plant.

Giraffe—These are the world's tallest animals. Some are eighteen feet tall, with necks measuring six and a half feet. They usually sleep standing up but are able to lie down. Giraffes can run at thirty or more miles per hour to get away from lions—the only real enemy of adult giraffes. If they have to, giraffes can defend themselves by kicking with their feet.

Great Rift valley—A great fissure in the earth's crust, the Great Rift valley is thousands of miles long. It was formed by a violent geological force that tore apart the earth's crust. The rift stretches south from the Red Sea, across Ethiopia, Kenya, and Tanzania. The walls on both sides are often 1500 feet high, and the width of the rift varies from thirty to three hundred miles.

Hippopotamus—One of the most dangerous animals in Africa, the hippopotamus has a huge, gaping mouth, and its jaw has two ivory tusks that can be as long as four feet. The tusks can cut through some of the toughest stems and roots of plants like a scythe. A hippopotamus usually weighs over a ton and can move at twenty miles per hour. It lives in swampy areas and can stay underwater for up to ten minutes.

Ivory—The creamy white material of the tusks of elephants and a few other animals like the hippopotamus and the walrus. Ivory is hard but easy to carve. It takes a high polish. The best ivory comes from African elephants and is a highly valued substance, being one of the main raw materials for craftsmen around the world. This has led to a serious depletion of the herds of wild elephants. Conservation attempts are now being made, in Kenya and elsewhere, to limit the killing of elephants for their ivory.

Kikuyu—The largest and most powerful ethnic group in Kenya (formerly British East Africa). The

Kikuyus spearheaded the drive for Kenyan independence. The first president of Kenya was a Kikuyu named Jomo Kenyatta.

Laibon—The Laibon are the hereditary priests of the Maasai. They mediate between the Maasai and Ngai, the god of their strictly monotheistic religion. The Maasai believe the Laibon can predict the future by throwing pebbles, like dice, on the ground.

Lake Naivasha—One of a chain of lakes in the Great Rift valley (see page 112). It is about thirty miles northwest of Nairobi. Its shallow waters are filled with papyrus plants and inhabited by herds of hippopotamuses.

Lake Victoria—The largest lake in Africa, and the second-largest freshwater lake in the world (exceeded only by Lake Superior, one of the five Great Lakes on the border between the United States and Canada). Lake Victoria lies partly in Kenya and partly in Tanzania and Uganda. It is roughly the size of Scotland and is the source of the Nile River in Egypt.

Lion—A big, powerful member of the cat family. Lions live mostly on grassy plains in areas with scrub trees. Their main food is deer, antelope, zebra, and other hoofed animals. They can see well in the dark and hunt mostly at night. Lions catch an animal about every four or five days and stuff themselves while they can. Only the males have the characteristic manes, the collars of thick hair around their heads. A good-sized lion can weigh five hundred pounds and be nine feet long from the tip of its nose to the end of its tail.

Lunatic Express—This was a nickname for the Uganda Railroad built by the British in the 1890s. It followed a six-hundred-mile route from the port of Mombasa in British East Africa to Lake Victoria, the source of the Nile River, in Uganda. It took six years of backbreaking effort to lay the tracks across waterless deserts, jagged volcanic wastelands, broad plains teeming with animals, and the Great Rift valley, a huge depression half a mile deep. Because of this, and other difficulties, such as attacks on the workers by lions and tropical diseases, the Uganda Railroad was nicknamed the Lunatic Express, because many people felt that only a "lunatic" could have thought to build it.

Maasai (also spelled Masai)—Nomadic tribes of East Africa that wander with their herds throughout the year. The Maasai subsist on the milk and blood of their cattle. Their temporary *kraal*, or "corral," consists of a large circular fence of thornbush with a ring of mud huts inside. The cattle are kept, when not grazing, at the center. Their warriors, the moran, were for many centuries the fierce raiders of East Africa (see below).

Moran—The warrior caste of the Maasai. The moran cover themselves with red ocher and body paint. Their headdresses are made from lion manes and vulture feathers. They carry large ox-hide shields and spears seven or eight feet long and hunt lions to get manes for their warbonnets.

Mount Kenya—A long-extinct volcano with several peaks covered with snow. Mount Kenya lies slightly south of the equator. Its highest peak is 17,058 feet high. The higher slopes are covered with forest preserves, while the fertile lower slopes are cultivated by the Kikuyu.

Mount Kilimanjaro—A largely extinct volcano, although there is some residual volcanic activity. Mount Kilimanjaro is just south of the Kenya-Tanzania border in Tanzania. Its central cone, Kibo, rises to 19,340 feet, the highest point in Africa, and is covered with ice and snow two hundred feet deep. Mount Kilimanjaro is the highest isolated mountain in the world (meaning it is not in a range or chain).

Nairobi—The capital of Kenya (succeeding Mombasa in 1905). It is situated about 330 miles northwest of the port of Mombasa. Originally a swampy area, the name Nairobi in the Maasai language means "place of cold water," or "sweet water for cattle," in another translation. Starting as an outlying trading station, it grew by leaps and bounds once it was reached by the railroad. Today it is as modern as New York City, with skyscrapers and luxury hotels.

Rhinoceros—One of the largest animals, the rhinoceros can weigh over three tons and stand six feet tall. It lives on the dry plain covered with tall brush. It eats grass and shrubs. The African rhinoceros has two horns. The front horn, used for defending itself, can be three feet long. The other, shorter horn is used for digging up bushes and small trees so that the rhinoceros can eat the leaves. Rhinoceroses are very nearsighted and can charge unpredictably.

Rickshaw (also spelled jinrikisha or jinrikshaw)—A two-wheeled "human-powered" vehicle. A rickshaw has a doorless, chairlike body with a collapsible hood and can carry one or two passengers. It is pulled by a man between two shafts in front. It was originally used in Japan, but its use spread to other areas of the Orient and Africa.

Roosevelt, Kermit (1889–1943)—The third of Theodore Roosevelt's six children (he had two girls and four boys). Kermit grew up in Theodore Roosevelt's Long Island home of Sagamore Hill. Kermit entered Harvard University shortly before going off to Africa with his father. He was a skilled photographer. At the start of World War I, Kermit obtained a staff position with the British forces in Mesopotamia where he won the British Military Cross for bravery. He later served in France with his younger brother, Ted, as a captain of artillery. At the beginning of World War II, Kermit again obtained a commission with the British Army but was soon forced to resign because of a heart condition.

Roosevelt, Theodore (1858–1919)—Writer, explorer, soldier, rancher, and twenty-sixth president of the United States during the years 1901 to 1909. In 1898, when the US declared war on Spain, Roosevelt resigned as assistant secretary of the navy and recruited a cavalry regiment that became known as the "Rough Riders." After Roosevelt led his men in a charge at the Battle of San Juan Hill, he became a national hero. He then served as governor of New York State and was later elected vice president under McKinley. Six months later, McKinley was assassinated, and Roosevelt became president. In 1904, Roosevelt was elected president in his own right. A crusader for public interest, he was hated by Big Business. Roosevelt also helped mediate the Russo-Japanese War and won the Noble Peace Prize. After leaving the presidency in 1909, he sailed for Africa with his son, Kermit, to collect specimens for the Smithsonian Institution in Washington.

Safari—An organized hunt to kill (or sometimes to photograph) wild animals in Africa. Safaris are usually put together by companies that provide guides and professional hunters as well as the supporting staff of cooks and other helpers. Nowadays, African countries closely supervise and regulate the number and the type of animals that can be killed. It is interesting to note that Theodore Roosevelt's various safaris usually consisted of around 250 porters, cooks, game skinners, gun bearers, and guides. There were also about sixty tents and a large number of wagons, many carrying the tons of salt needed for preserving the animal skins. All in all, Roosevelt collected fourteen thousand specimens of animals, birds, reptiles, and fish.

Smithsonian Institution—An institution of learning and research founded in 1829 by James Smithson. It is located in Washington, DC, and funds scientific research and expeditions such as Theodore Roosevelt's. Its buildings also house exhibits of all kinds.

Swahili—A language developed along the coast of East Africa from elements of the native Bantu language as well as Arabic and Persian. The word

"Swahili" comes from the Arabic *sahil*, meaning coast. It was, and is, used as a *lingua franca*—universal language—for much of Africa.

Wildebeest (also called a gnu)—An African antelope that is the most abundant grazing animal in the wilds of East Africa. Wildebeest live in large herds that are almost continually on the move. They are higher at the shoulder (where they stand three to four feet high) than at the tail. Both sexes have horns that grow forward and turn up at the tips.

Zebra—A striped, horselike animal, the zebra has parallel black (or brown) stripes on a white background. The stripes evolved as camouflage to help them hide, mostly from lions. Zebras are more stubborn and not as gentle as horses and are difficult to train.

Suggested Reading

If you enjoyed this book, here are some other books on Africa that you might like:

Amin, Mohamed. *Cradle of Mankind*. Woodstock, New York: The Overlook Press, 1983. This book documents the life of the different tribes of northern Kenya and neighboring countries around Lake Turkana, the largest lake in the Great Rift valley. Recent discoveries suggest that this area is the birthplace of humankind. The book is quite well done and illustrated with splendid color photographs.

Beard, Peter H. *The End of the Game*. San Francisco: Chronicle Books, 1988. This book tells the story of how explorers, missionaries, and big-game hunters like Theodore Roosevelt in their quest for adventure changed the face of Africa. It also examines the complex relationships between humans and animals in Africa. It is illustrated with over three hundred photographs.

Brown, Leslie. *Africa*. New York: Random House, 1965. This large, thick, and overwhelmingly illustrated book covers all the areas of Africa—from the Sahara, across the Congo rain forests, the plains of Kenya, and the Great Rift valley to its most southern tip. It shows how Africa is one of the most varied places on earth.

East Africa. Amsterdam: Time-Life Books, 1986. This well-illustrated book follows the history and customs of the peoples of East Africa. It documents their successes and their tragedies, from the beginning of humankind to the latest political upheavals.

McCullough, David. *Mornings on Horseback.* New York: Simon and Schuster, 1981. This book tells the story of the young Theodore Roosevelt, a sickly little boy, handicapped by nearly fatal attacks of asthma, and his struggle to adulthood. It covers the seventeen years from when Roosevelt was ten years old to his return from the West as a hardened cowboy.

Miller, Charles. *The Lunatic Express.* New York: The Macmillan Company, 1971. This is the gripping story of the colossal six-year struggle to build a railroad over six hundred miles of barely explored territory. It was a struggle that was to cost countless lives from derailments, disease, Maasai raids, and the attacks of lions, earning it the name "Lunatic Express." It is also the story of the colonization of East Africa by the English.

Shachtman, Tom. *Growing Up Masai.* New York: Macmillan Publishing Co., 1981. This childrens' book is illustrated with excellent black and white photos, strikingly documenting the life of the Maasai—a way of life that has remained unchanged for a thousand years.

Willock, Colin. *Africa's Rift Valley.* Amsterdam: Time-Life Books, 1975. Like the Time-Life book on East Africa (cited above), this marvelously illustrated and well-printed book gives a comprehensive picture of the geology, wildlife, history, and culture of the region. Both have beautiful color photos.

ABOUT THE AUTHOR

RICHARD BRIGHTFIELD is a graduate of Johns Hopkins University, where he studied biology, psychology, and archaeology. For many years he worked as a graphic designer at Columbia University. He has written many books in the Choose Your Own Adventure series, including *Master of Kung Fu*, *Master of Tae Kwon Do*, *Hijacked!*, *Master of Karate*, and *Master of the Martial Arts*. In addition, Mr. Brightfield is the coauthor of the first four books in The Young Indiana Jones Chronicles series. He has also coauthored more than a dozen game books with his wife, Glory. The Brightfields and their daughter, Savitri, now live on the coast of southern Florida.

ABOUT THE ILLUSTRATOR

FRANK BOLLE studied at Pratt Institute. He has worked as an illustrator for many national magazines and now creates and draws cartoons for magazines as well. He has also worked in advertising and children's educational materials and has drawn and collaborated on several newspaper comic strips, including *Annie* and *Winnie Winkle*. He has illustrated many books in the Choose Your Own Adventure series, most recently *The Lost Ninja*, *Daredevil Park*, *Kidnapped!*, *The Terrorist Trap*, *Ghost Train*, *Magic Master* and *Master of the Martial Arts*. He is also the illustrator of the first four books in The Young Indiana Jones Chronicles series. A native of Brooklyn Heights, New York, Mr. Bolle now lives and works in Westport, Connecticut.

CHOOSE YOUR OWN ADVENTURE

- ☐ 26965-8 **CAVE OF TIME #1** $3.25
- ☐ 27393-0 **JOURNEY UNDER THE SEA #2** $3.25
- ☐ 26593-8 **DANGER IN THE DESERT #3** $2.99
- ☐ 27453-8 **SPACE AND BEYOND #4** $3.25
- ☐ 27419-8 **CURSE OF THE HAUNTED MANSION #5** $2.99
- ☐ 27053-2 **VAMPIRE EXPRESS #31** $2.99
- ☐ 26983-6 **GHOST HUNTER #52** $2.99
- ☐ 27565-8 **SECRET OF THE NINJA #66** $2.99
- ☐ 26723-X **SPACE VAMPIRE #71** $2.99
- ☐ 27063-X **FIRST OLYMPICS, THE #77** $3.25
- ☐ 27718-9 **MASTER OF KUNG FU #88** $2.99
- ☐ 27968-8 **RETURN OF THE NINJA #92** $3.25
- ☐ 28009-0 **CAPTIVE #93** $2.50
- ☐ 28155-0 **YOU ARE A GENIUS #95** $3.25
- ☐ 28294-8 **STOCK CAR CHAMPION #96** $3.25
- ☐ 28440-1 **THROUGH THE BLACK HOLE #97** $3.25
- ☐ 28351-0 **YOU ARE A MILLIONAIRE #98** $3.25
- ☐ 28316-2 **WORST DAY OF YOUR LIFE #100** $3.25

Bantam Books, Dept. AV, 2451 South Wolf Road, Des Plaines, IL 60018

Please send me the items I have checked above. I am enclosing $ ____
(please add $2.50 to cover postage and handling). Send check or money
order, no cash or C.O.D.s please.

Mr/Ms _____

Address _____

City/State _____ Zip_____

AV–2/93

Please allow four to six weeks for delivery.
Prices and availability subject to change without notice.

Join The Adventure!

There's a world of adventure awaiting you when you join the official Lucasfilm Fan Club!

Go behind-the-scenes on the new television series *The Young Indiana Jones Chronicles* in each issue of the quarterly Lucasfilm Fan Club Magazine. Exclusive interviews with the cast and crew, exciting full-color photos and more fill every page! In addition, the latest news on the new *Star Wars* movies is found within the pages of the Lucasfilm Fan Club Magazine as well as interviews with actors, directors, producers, etc. from past Lucasfilm productions, special articles and photos on the special effects projects at Industrial Light & Magic and more! Plus you'll receive, with each issue, our exclusive Lucasfilm Merchandise catalog filled with all the latest hard-to-find collectibles from *Star Wars* to *The Young Indiana Jones Chronicles* including special offers for fan club members only!

When you join, you'll receive a 1 year subscription to the magazine plus our exclusive membership kit which includes:

- Full-color poster of 16 year-old Indy, Sean Patrick Flanery!
- Full-color poster of 9 year-old Indy, Corey Carrier!
- *Young Indiana Jones Chronicles* Book Sticker!
- *Young Indiana Jones Chronicles* Patch!
- Welcome Letter From George Lucas!
- Lucasfilm Fan Club Membership Card!

AND MORE!

Don't miss this opportunity to be a part of the adventure and excitement that Lucasfilm creates! Join The Lucasfilm Fan Club today!

MEMBERSHIP FOR ONE YEAR
$9.95-US, $12.00-CAN., $21.95-FOR.

Send check, money order or Mastercard/Visa order to:
The Lucasfilm Fan Club
P.O. Box 111000
Aurora, Colorado 80042 USA

Copyright ©1992 Lucasfilm Ltd.

DA50 7/92

A CHOOSE YOUR OWN ADVENTURE® BOOK

PASSPORT

THE NEWS TEAM THAT COVERS THE WORLD

YOU MAKE THE NEWS!

You are an anchor for the Passport news team.
Together with Jake, your cameraman, and Eddy,
an investigative journalist, you travel the world on
assignment, covering firsthand some of the hottest
events in the news.